To: EMILY

WHEN YOU WILL BE A LITTLE
OLDER I HOPE THAT YOU
WILL WALK WITH ME BY
THE CANAL AND ENJOY
SEEING THERE ANIMALS.

LOVE,

AUNT VERONICA

CATHRYN FALWELL

Scoot!

Greenwillow Books
An Imprint of HarperCollinsPublishers

Paper collages were used to prepare the full-color art.
The text type is Poor Richard Opti.

Library of Congress Cataloging-in-Publication Data
Falwell, Cathryn, (date).
Scoot! / by Cathryn Falwell.
  p. cm.
"Greenwillow Books."
Summary: Six silent turtles sit still as stones on a log, as energetic movement
by the other animals in the pond happens all around them.
ISBN-13: 978-0-06-128882-1 (trade bdg.) ISBN-10: 0-06-128882-9 (trade bdg.)
ISBN-13: 978-0-06-128883-8 (lib. bdg.) ISBN-10: 0-06-128883-7 (lib. bdg.)
[1. Turtles—Fiction. 2. Pond animals—Fiction. 3. Stories in rhyme—Fiction.] I. Title.
PZ8.3.F2163 Sc 2008 [E]—dc22 2007018355

First Edition 10 9 8 7 6 5 4 3 2 1

Greenwillow Books

For my dad,
Warren Falwell,
who sent me outside to play

Down at the pond
on a sunny
summer day . . .
six silent turtles
sit
still
as
stones.

Green frogs
leap.

Beetles
creep.

Herons lurch.

Finches perch.

scoot!

On
every
rock
and
leaf
and
root!

But the six
silent turtles
sit still
as stones.

Wood ducks glide.

Water striders slide.

Salamanders dash.

Tadpoles splash.

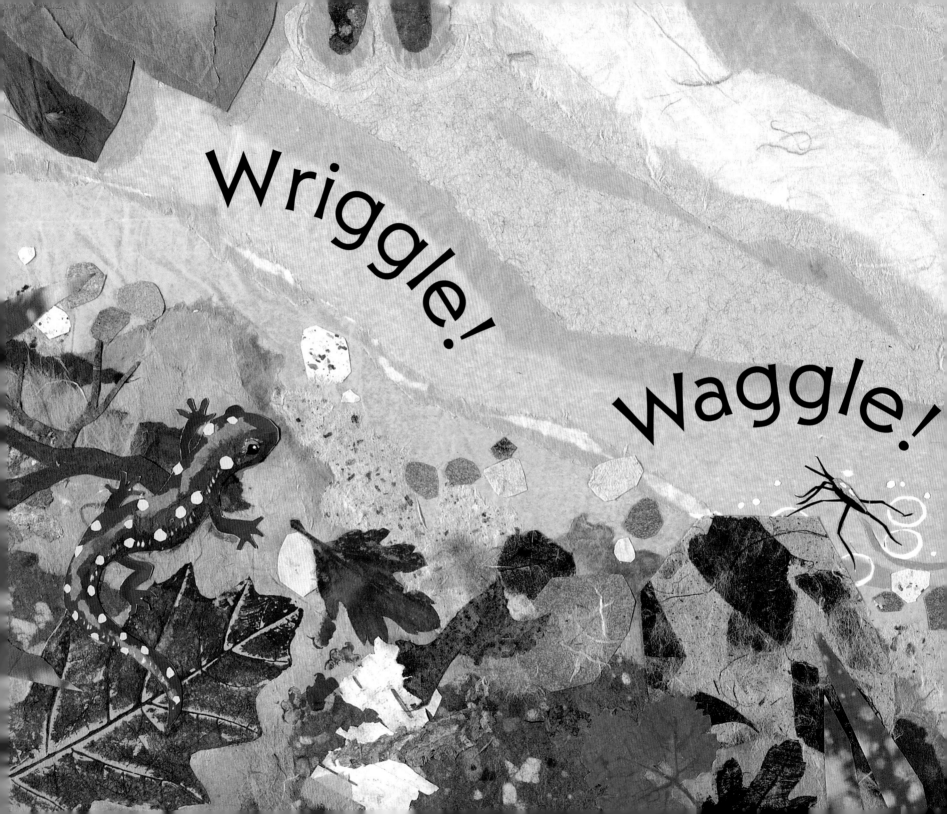

Scuttle!

Skim!

On every reed and stone and limb!

But the six silent turtles
sit still as stones.

Spiders swing.

Dragonflies zing.

Red squirrels
hurry.

Chipmunks
scurry.

Flitter! Flee!

On every branch and shrub and tree!

But then . . . strong winds blow.

Pond waves grow.

Fern fronds rustle.

Butterflies bustle.

And the six startled turtles . . .

. . . suddenly **speed** away!

Down at the pond
on a sunny
summer day!

Notes from Frog Song Pond

From my tree house I can see many dashing, scampering, scooting creatures. Life on the pond is very busy, but the turtles are quiet and still on their log, basking in the sun.

← note: black + white stripes

Eastern painted turtles

Chipmunks have cheek pouches for carrying seeds, nuts, and other foods to their burrows.

Dragonflies are speedy fliers. They have four wings and can fly forward and backward. They can also hover in midair.

Water striders' legs are covered with waterproof hair. This lets them skate across the surface of the pond. ↓

A great blue heron is able to curl its neck into an S shape because it has special bones. The heron's neck is like a spring. When the heron spots a fish, it can strike quickly. ↘

dragonfly

ladybug beetles

goldfinch & house finch

water strider

bullfrog tadpoles

chipmunk

great blue heron

Wood ducks are amazing! They make their nests in hollow spaces in trees, often high above the ground. The tiny newly hatched ducklings leap from the nest when they are just one day old, and follow their mother to the water.

oak leaf print

The female black and yellow garden spider is also known as the "writing spider," because the series of zigzags she makes in the middle of her web looks like handwriting.

While walking in the woods, I found a broken, empty wasp nest on the ground. Wasps made this nest by chewing plant fibers and mixing them with their saliva. This creates a material that is like paper. I used pieces of the nest to make some of the tree bark in this book.

wasp nest in tree

birch bark

wasp nest "paper"

black & yellow garden spider

wood ducks

red-backed salamander

green frog

red squirrel

tiger swallowtail

white admiral

Printing Textures

Pour a small amount of paint onto an old plate or bowl. Dip an object carefully into the paint, or use a brush to apply the paint to the object. Press onto paper.

Try different color combinations!

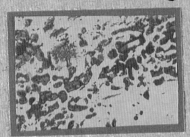 tree bark

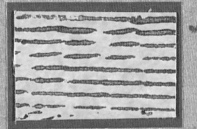 corrugated cardboard

 broccoli flower

 Bubble Wrap

 broccoli stem

 new pencil eraser

 cut carrot

 plastic wrap